Acting Edition

Birthday Candles

by Noah Haidle

I0591852

ıⅡSAMUEL FRENCHⅡı

ISBN 978-0-573-71007-0

www.concordtheatricals.com
www.concordtheatricals.co.uk

FOR PRODUCTION INQUIRIES

UNITED STATES AND CANADA
info@concordtheatricals.com
1-866-979-0447

UNITED KINGDOM AND EUROPE
licensing@concordtheatricals.co.uk
020-7054-7298

Each title is subject to availability from Concord Theatricals Corp.,
depending upon country of performance. Please be aware that
BIRTHDAY CANDLES may not be licensed by Concord Theatricals
Corp. in your territory. Professional and amateur producers should
contact the nearest Concord Theatricals Corp. office or licensing
partner to verify availability.

This work is published by Samuel French, an imprint of Concord
Theatricals Corp.

BIRTHDAY CANDLES was originally commissioned and produced by Detroit Public Theatre, Detroit MI. Producing Artistic Directors: Courtney Burkett, Sarah Clare Corporandy and Sarah Winkler. Developed as part of Chautauqua Theater Company's New Play Workshop series, 2017, underwritten by the Roe Green Foundation. Originally produced on Broadway in 2022 by Roundabout Theatre Company, New York. The performance was directed by Vivienne Benesch, Associate Director Katherine McGerr, Scenic Designer Christine Jones, Associate Set Designer Andrews Moerdyk, Costume Designer Toni-Leslie James, Lighting Designer Jen Schriever, Sound Designer John Gromada, Company Manager Kathryn McCumber, Vocal Coach Kate Wilson, original music by Kate Hopgood. The cast was as follows:

ERNESTINE ASHWORTH . . . . Debra Messing

ALICE / MADELINE / ERNIE . . . . Susannah Flood

KENNETH . . . . Enrico Colantoni

MATT / WILLIAM . . . . John Earl Jelks

BILLY / JOHN . . . . Christopher Livingston

JOAN / ALEX / BETH . . . . Crystal Finn

CHARACTERS

(in order of appearance)

Twelve roles, six actors, one goldfish

ERNESTINE ASHWORTH – Travels from age seven to one hundred and seven. In that time she will be a daughter, a girlfriend, a wife, a mother, a friend, an aunt, a mother-in-law, a widow, a second wife, a grandmother, a great grandmother, and a great-great grandmother.

ALICE – Selfless. Strong. Ernestine's mother.

KENNETH – Ernestine's awkward and annoying next door neighbor.

MATT – Chiseled jawline. A middle linebacker on the high school football team. Ernestine's boyfriend then husband.

BILLY – Sensitive. An ear for music. Ernestine and Matt's son.

MADELINE – Troubled. Bemused. Beautiful. Erudite. Ernestine and Matt's daughter. Played by actor playing Alice.

JOAN – Anxious. Very anxious. Billy's wife.

ALEX – Takes no bullshit. Billy and Joan's daughter. Played by actor playing Joan.

ERNIE – Ethereal. Vivacious. She doesn't walk, she glides. Alex's daughter. Played by actor playing Alice and Madeline.

WILLIAM – Thirteen. Grand. Played by actor playing Matt.

JOHN – A man woken up in the middle of the night. Played by actor playing Billy.

BETH – John's domestic partner, she quit smoking ten years ago and hasn't been in a good mood since. Played by actor playing Joan and Alex.

SETTING

A kitchen in Grand Rapids, Michigan.
A working oven.
A goldfish in a bowl.

TIME

One hundred years and ninety minutes concurrently,
no breaks between scenes and no intermission.

AUTHOR'S NOTES

A line across the page like this one indicates that time has passed, at least a year, sometimes more. How this is to be indicated in the staging is open to many interpretations.

*On time

To give everything away, we're going to be traveling from Ernestine's seventeenth birthday to her one hundred and seventh. The years of the play are outside the confines of literal history, there are no correlations to actual past events in the timeline of the world, e.g., nobody is going to World War Two or walking on the moon.

**On acting older

Younger actors playing old characters is a ripe situation for wonkiness. Canes, hobbling, wigs, shaky hands, ear trumpets, gravelly commands, "Speak up, sonny!" You know what I'm talking about. Please don't fall into those traps.

Her transformation is much more inner than outer, the play doesn't legislate how her transformation takes place or the age of the actress, which could be from sixteen to one hundred (call me if you are able to hire anyone over ninety seven). There is a legitimate version where she never plays age at all, allowing the audience to simply project the passing of time onto her, and I suppose there is the possibility for canes, hobbling, wigs and shaky hands. Yes, that's contradicting myself, but any technique is perfect if it's performed with grace.

***On baking

Yes, you're going to have to bake a cake onstage. Give yourself lots of time to choreograph the baking, figure out the temperament of the onstage oven, of the altitude of the theater (cakes rise differently at higher altitudes), of getting used to the oven mitts, the idiosyncrasies of the mixer, etcetera. If the cake doesn't come out perfect during the performance it's no big deal, the play isn't about winning a cake decorating contest. What is essential is the reality of the endeavor. The audience must see the actual effort of making the cake. See the flour flying, see the eggs beating beaten, smell the sugar browning. Without this grounded act, the telescoping of one hundred years loses its anchor and becomes simply fantasy.

****A recipe

Yes, there are tons of cake recipes out there, and while in your private life you want to create an extravaganza, for the purposes of sanity and theatricality, a simple butter cake is probably the best way to go. They take about twenty minutes to prep, they cook for thirty, and cool for another twenty or more, which are great for a play transpiring in real time. Here's the recipe for the 'Birthday Candles Real Time Golden Butter Cake.'

1 cup white sugar
½ cup butter
2 eggs,
2 teaspoons vanilla extract
1 ½ cups all-purpose flour,
1 ¾ teaspoons baking powder,
½ cup milk

Preheat oven the 350 degrees. Grease and flour a 9x9 pan. Cream together sugar and butter. Beat in the eggs, one at a time, then stir in the vanilla. Combine flour and baking powder, add to the creamed mixture. Stir in the milk until the batter is smooth. Spoon batter into the pan. Bake for thirty minutes, when it springs to the touch, we're done. (There is a lot of room to run concerning icing, pastry bags, and all the rest, but don't even think about it until you have the choreography and timing of the basic cake making down pat).

All mankind is of one author and is one volume: when one man dies, one chapter is not torn out of the book, but translated into a better language; and every chapter must be so translated as God's hand is in every translation, and his hand shall bind up all our scattered leaves again for the library where every book shall lie open to one another.

John Donne

For my wife

(Evening.)

(Close to sunset.)

(A kitchen in Grand Rapids, Michigan.)

(Like many other kitchens.)

ERNESTINE. Have I wasted my life?

ALICE. You're seventeen.

ERNESTINE. In the career of my soul, how many times have I turned from wonder?

ALICE. We'd better get started on the cake, goose, the guests will be arriving soon.

> **(ALICE** *begins to make the cake.)*

> **(ERNESTINE** *doesn't have any interest.)*

ERNESTINE. Two hundred and fifty babies are born every second.

ALICE. Unceasing life.

ERNESTINE. Fifteen thousand every hour.

ALICE. No rest.

ERNESTINE. In another week, two and a half million

How am I supposed to reconcile my individual existence against the weight of those numbers?

ALICE. Now come here and learn how to make this cake.

You're almost out of this house, Ernestine.

ALICE. Soon you'll have a family and I'd like you to remember something of me.

ERNESTINE. I won't be having a family.

ALICE. Let's have this conversation again in ten years.

ERNESTINE. I am a rebel against the universe.

I will wage war with the everyday.

I am going to surprise God!

ALICE. Eggs, butter, sugar, salt.

The humblest ingredients.

But when you turn back and look far enough, you see atoms left over from creation.

ERNESTINE. Stardust.

The machinery of the cosmos is all here, I get it.

Will you help me with my audition?

> (**ERNESTINE** *gives* **ALICE** *a dog-eared copy of King Lear.*)
>
> (**ALICE** *looks at it.*)

ALICE. No high school should perform King Lear, It's unholy.

ERNESTINE. Queen Lear.

A feminist interpretation.

From, 'Madam, do you know me?'

> (*Reads.*)

ALICE. *(As Cordelia.)* Madam, do you know me?

ERNESTINE. *(As Queen Lear.)* You are a spirit, I know.

When did you die?

ALICE. *(As Cordelia.)* Still, still, far wide!

ERNESTINE. 'Where have I been? Where am I?'

Wait.

Look!

A crown of flowers.

> (**ERNESTINE** *uses the colander for her crown of flowers.*)

ALICE. Rosemary.

ERNESTINE. And rue.

ALICE. Daffodils.

ERNESTINE. And chrysanthemums.

ALICE. Gorgeous.

ERNESTINE. Again.

From, Madam, do you know me?

ALICE. *(As Cordelia.)* Madam, do you know me?

ERNESTINE. *(As Queen Lear.)* You are a spirit, I know. When did you die?

ALICE. *(As Cordelia.)* Still, still, far wide!

> *(Watch out,* **ERNESTINE** *is incredible.)*

ERNESTINE. *(As Queen Lear.)* Where have I been? Where am I? Fair daylight.

I am mightily abused. I should even die with pity.

To see another thus. I know not what to say.

I will not swear these are my hands. Let's see.

I feel this pin prick. Would I were assured

Of my condition.

(Pause.)

(ALICE *beams at her daughter.)*

ERNESTINE. That's your line.

I'll give it to you again.

(As Queen Lear.) I feel this pin prick. Would I were assured

Of my condition.

ALICE. I am so proud of you, Ernestine.

ERNESTINE. Mom!!!

ALICE. Just let me look at you.

Strong and beautiful.

Talented beyond.

ERNESTINE. Do you think I'll get the part?

Because if Donna Kaplan gets the lead in another school play I'll die.

ALICE. You were born to play it.

ERNESTINE. You promise?

ALICE. Donna Kaplan cry your eyes out.

> **(ERNESTINE** *does a small dance of excitement and nervousness.)*

Time for measurements.

ERNESTINE. Not this year.

ALICE. Every year.

> **(ALICE** *pushes* **ERNESTINE** *to stand against the wall where there are different lines measuring heights from different years.)*

Shoes.

Straighten up.

(**ERNESTINE** *straightens up.*)

Ernestine.

Aged seventeen.

Seventeen years ago today I got to meet you and I don't understand the journey from then to here.

A second ago I washed you in this sink.

In this sink, looking out over the field.

Just this view.

My whole life.

The same trees, grass, flowers, the same angle of the sun.

(**ALICE** *begins to cry.*)

ERNESTINE. Mom, what's wrong?

ALICE. Hold my hand?

(**ERNESTINE** *holds her mother's hand.*)

ERNESTINE. I won't let go until you do.

ALICE. Risk your heart.

Find your place in the universe.

Do that for me.

ERNESTINE. I promise.

ALICE. I wish you so many beautiful hours.

(*A rest.*)

(*They hold hands.*)

ERNESTINE. Let's start the cake, Mom.

ALICE. You're right.

ERNESTINE. The genius of a party is to offer people a rest.

ALICE. You have been listening.

ERNESTINE. A rest from the daily human errand to travel morning until night.

ALICE. That's right.

ERNESTINE. A song.

A wish.

A breath.

ALICE. And then home.

*(**ALICE** steps out of herself, out of the play.)*

*(She watches **ERNESTINE** for a moment and then exits.)*

(One year later.)

*(**ERNESTINE** begins to start the cake.)*

*(**KENNETH** enters carrying a wrapped goldfish bowl, unseen by **ERNESTINE**.)*

*(He doesn't want to scare **ERNESTINE**, but doesn't want to yell, either.)*

(He decides the best way is to walk slowly toward her and wave when she's in sight of him.)

(She turns.)

ERNESTINE. Ahhhhhh!!!!

KENNETH. Ahhhhh!!!

ERNESTINE. Kenneth!

KENNETH. I'm sorry!

ERNESTINE. You've got to stop doing that!

KENNETH. I was trying to stop doing that!!!

ERNESTINE. An eighteen-year old boy and you can't make an entrance.

KENNETH. An 18.2917-year old young man and I'll do better next time, I promise.

ERNESTINE. The party isn't for two hours.

KENNETH. I thought maybe I could help with the cake.

ERNESTINE. No, you can't.

KENNETH. Then I thought maybe I could keep you company.

ERNESTINE. You could, but I don't want you to.

KENNETH. Ouch.

ERNESTINE. Two hours, Kenneth.

KENNETH. Hey, did I forget to tell you that your Queen Lear was triumphant?

ERNESTINE. It was sweet of you to see all eight performances.

KENNETH. I snuck out of an emergency root canal so I could see the Sunday matinee and passed out for the third act but was able to rally in time for the heath scene.

ERNESTINE. My Mom only saw one.

KENNETH. Opening night?

ERNESTINE. No, she was too sick.

KENNETH. The Sunday matinee?

ERNESTINE. Closing night.

KENNETH. Triumphant.

Magisterial.

She couldn't have seen a better performance.

ERNESTINE. I hate when people pretend it didn't happen, or say inane things like 'If there's anything I can do.'

KENNETH. Yeah. There is.

Bring her back.

ERNESTINE. Right.

Bring her back.

(*Silence.*)

KENNETH. People say I have terrible timing, but do you want to go to prom with me?

ERNESTINE. Kenneth.

KENNETH. You already told me no twice, so why would I ask again, right?

ERNESTINE. Insanity.

KENNETH. Hope.

ERNESTINE. No.

A million, trillion times, I will never go to the prom with you.

KENNETH. So I should stop asking, is what I'm hearing.

ERNESTINE. Go home until the party, Kenneth.

KENNETH. But I have to set up pin the tail on the donkey.

ERNESTINE. Which I don't want to play.

KENNETH. But I'll just be next door sitting on the edge of my bed, waiting to come back.

ERNESTINE. Then you'll have something to look forward to.

KENNETH. Will you open my present before I go?

ERNESTINE. Solely because I'm a generous person, yes.

(She opens the present voraciously.)

(A goldfish swimming in a bowl.)

KENNETH. It's a goldfish.

ERNESTINE. I see that.

KENNETH. You did that incredibly well presented and illuminating report on the memory span of a goldfish in school and I thought perhaps you might like to own one yourself.

ERNESTINE. I said that goldfish have a three second memory span and that without a sense of history life would cease to have meaning.

KENNETH. Whoops.

I'll just take him back to the pet store where he'll die a horribly painful death.

ERNESTINE. They'll kill him?

KENNETH. Worse. Atman is what those of us in the pet industry know as a feeder fish. Larger carnivorous fish eat him for dinner. Or lunch. Or between meals. Late-night snacks. Food chain. Circle of life, and whatnot.

ERNESTINE. Atman.

KENNETH. A Sanskrit word for self.

But not a personal self, but as the divinity within yourself.

ERNESTINE. Hell of a name for a goldfish.

KENNETH. Go big or go home.

The Katha Upanishad is the first to use the concept of Atman as a beginning argument of achieving liberation from human suffering.

KENNETH. I quote and please forgive my basic translation:

'Like fire spreads itself throughout the world and takes the shape of that which it burns, the internal Atman of all living beings, while remaining one fire, takes the form of what He enters and is at the same time outside all forms.'

(Pause for effect.)

Anywho, I'll get him out of your way and to his execution.

ERNESTINE. Atman can stay.

For the time being.

(They watch Atman swim.)

KENNETH. You said goldfish only have a three-second long memory span.

Can you imagine that?

Three.

Two.

One.

Boom.

Then the world begins anew.

(They watch Atman swim.)

ERNESTINE. I miss her.

I don't understand the world without my Mom.

Every day takes me further away from her, from her voice, telling me everything will be okay.

KENNETH. Just checking in, but you're still sure you don't want to go to prom with me.

ERNESTINE. Stop, Kenneth, you're embarrassing yourself.

KENNETH. But I don't feel embarrassed.

ERNESTINE. Go.

KENNETH. See you in one hour and fity six minutes. One hour and fifty five minutes and fifty nine seconds, fifty eight seconds, fifty seven ...

> (**KENNETH** *leaves.*)

ERNESTINE. Hello, Atman.

I'm Ernestine Ashworth, nice to meet you.

Or I guess to meet the divinity within myself.

It's my birthday.

> (**MATT** *enters, unseen by* **ERNESTINE.***)*

> (*He watches.*)

I'm eighteen.

I'm eighteen today and this is my proclamation.

I will get out of this town and pilgrimage toward finding my place in the scale of the universe.

You are my witness.

MATT. Hey.

ERNESTINE. Go away!

MATT. Sorry.

ERNESTINE. Matt.

MATT. I'm too early.

ERNESTINE. No no no. Matt, you're right on time.

I was just starting my cake.

My mother made it every year for my birthday.

This ritual, these gestures, is one way I can keep her alive.

MATT. This must be hard. Your first birthday. Without your mom.

If there's anything I can do.

ERNESTINE. That's so sweet, Matt.

MATT. Oh, hey, so I sorta got you this.

> *(A present that was in his pocket.)*

ERNESTINE. You didn't have to.

MATT. Yes, I did.

What asshole goes to a birthday party without a present?

> **(ERNESTINE** *laughs loudly to make* **MATT** *feel good about his joke.)*
>
> *(She wipes her hands off and opens the present.)*

A blue ribbon.

ERNESTINE. I see that.

MATT. Remember when you said you stole a piece of blue ribbon at the drugstore but gave it back immediately out of overwhelming guilt?

ERNESTINE. That was when I was six, I can't believe you remembered.

MATT. In keeping with the spirit of the thing, I also stole it from the drugstore.

ERNESTINE. I think it would look nice in my hair.

MATT. I think it would look stunning.

> *(She puts it in her hair.)*

ERNESTINE. And?

MATT. I was right.

ERNESTINE. You could help me with the cake if you wanted.

MATT. It would be my honor.

ERNESTINE. Take this apron. I wore it until I inherited my mom's.

(*She gives him an apron.*)

MATT. Could you help tie it?

Sorry.

ERNESTINE. Don't be.

(*She helps tie the apron.*)

MATT. My hands.

Like porterhouse steaks.

ERNESTINE. Better for holding what you want to hold.

MATT. What?

ERNESTINE. Oh golly.

We better get started on the cake.

MATT. Hey, you want to go to prom with me?

ERNESTINE. Like as your date?

MATT. No, like as my sister, yes as my date.

ERNESTINE. No.

MATT. Yeah, I was probably not going to go anyway.

ERNESTINE. It's not personal.

MATT. How is it not personal?

ERNESTINE. I'm not going to prom with you or anybody.

We're about to graduate high school, Matt.

ERNESTINE. Grand Rapids, Michigan? The Midwest?

No, thanks, there's the world.

I'm not falling in love with you or anyone else.

MATT. I didn't ask you to fall in love with me.

ERNESTINE. We go to the prom.

Dance all night.

I bury my head in your shoulders and think you are my home.

And then the back of some car, liquor on our breath, trying to get in my pants.

MATT. Not true!

ERNESTINE. You don't find me attractive?

MATT. Incredibly!

ERNESTINE. Two by two, that's how we're meant to travel through this life, right, I'm denying human nature, huh?

MATT. I'm confused.

ERNESTINE. I agree.

MATT. I'm not asking you to travel through this life.

I'm asking you to the prom!

(She kisses him hard.)

ERNESTINE. No weddings or birthings or dyings not here not me.

MATT. Okay.

ERNESTINE. I am a rebel against the universe.

I am waging a war with the everyday.

I am going to surprise God!

MATT. Okay.

(*He touches her hand tenderly.*)

(*She doesn't move it away.*)

(*Twenty one years later.*)

BILLY. (*Offstage.*) Mom!?!?!?!

ERNESTINE. What?!?!?!?!

BILLY. (*Offstage.*) Have I wasted my life?????

ERNESTINE. You're seventeen!!!

(**BILLY** *enters.*)

(*Seventeen years old.*)

BILLY. In the career of my soul, how many times have I turned from wonder?

ERNESTINE. I asked the same question when I was your age, goose.

BILLY. And then you stopped asking because the answers began to terrify you.

ERNESTINE. Let's have this conversation again in ten years.

BILLY. You're weak!

You fell into the ranks, joined the life of conformity.

ERNESTINE. Goose.

BILLY. Just because you gave up doesn't mean I will.

MATT. Billy, don't talk to your mother that way

BILLY. No, I'll talk to you that way instead.

You have no original impulse in your entire body.

How can you live with that?

MATT. Somehow I manage.

BILLY. It's not too late.

MATT. To do what?

BILLY. To breathe one second of authenticity before you die.

ERNESTINE. Your sister will be home soon. Can we call a truce for today?

MATT. Your generation should get up off your therapist's couch, knuckle up, and get to work.

We weren't there for you emotionally?

Let's share a good cry.

The world doesn't owe you free dinner.

Grow up.

BILLY. You're a shadow in a suit posing as a human, you should be ashamed of yourself.

> *(He goes off.)*
>
> *(Quiet.)*
>
> *(They bake the cake.)*
>
> *(Note: this is the last time the stage directions will indicate that* **ERNESTINE** *is baking her cake but she's pretty much always doing it.)*

ERNESTINE. On my birthday.

MATT. I'm sorry.

> *(They bake the cake.)*
>
> *(Okay, that was the last time.)*

ERNESTINE. Did we settle?

MATT. We chose.

ERNESTINE. Excuses.

MATT. Responsibilities.

ERNESTINE. The world is so big.

MATT. Tuition. The mortgage.

ERNESTINE. Just this view.

MATT. The business of living.

>*(Piano music in the other room.*)*

>*(It's their son, **BILLY**, He's not very good.)*

Money well spent on piano lessons.

ERNESTINE. He's getting better.

MATT. Very slowly.

>*(They listen to the piano music.)*

>*(Quiet.)*

ERNESTINE. Thirty-nine years old.

What have I done with my time?

MATT. We raised a family, Ernestine.

A beautiful family.

>*(**MATT** touches her hand tenderly but it's less soothing than it was when they were eighteen.)*

---

* **BILLY** *will play this same piano music over the years of the play, so rather than have the piece be a recital standard like Chopin or Bach, there is an opportunity to write an original theme for **BILLY** which will grow and die, mirroring the shape of his life.*

A license to produce BIRTHDAY CANDLES does not include a performance license for any third-party or copyrighted music. Licensees should create an original composition or use music in the public domain. For further information, please see Music Use Note on page 3.

*(**MADELINE** enters.)*

(Perpetually preoccupied.)

MADELINE. So sorry I'm late.

MATT. There's the college senior!

ERNESTINE. Madeline!

MADELINE. So sorry I'm late again.

MATT. There's the college graduate!

ERNESTINE. Madeline!

MADELINE. So sorry I'm late perpetually.

MATT. There's the unpaid intern!

ERNESTINE. Madeline, you made it, your father was getting so worried.

MATT. No I wasn't.

ERNESTINE. Just let me look at you.

For one second.

MATT. Maybe a little worried.

Come here, Maddy.

(He hugs her.)

(She's his favorite.)

MADELINE. I'm actually going by Athena right now.

ERNESTINE. Athena?

MADELINE. The goddess of wisdom?

Hello, read a book.

ERNESTINE. But it sounds nothing like your name.

MADELINE. And?

MATT. Nicknames usually sound like people's names.

MADELINE. It's not a nickname it's an alias.

Or a redefinition, more specifically.

ERNESTINE. We'll call you whatever you want we're just so glad you're home.

> (**BILLY** *enters.*)

BILLY. I'm going out.

Hi, Athena.

> (**BILLY** *goes toward the door.*)

ERNESTINE. Wait, Billy!

We don't see you.

BILLY. Because I don't live here.

MATT. Right.

Which is why we'd like to catch up.

BILLY. School is hard.

I drink too much, I worry about what everyone thinks, I generally feel like my light is dying.

We good?

ERNESTINE. Any girls we should know the name of?

MADELINE. Yeah, Billy, any girls we should know the name of?

ERNESTINE. What was your prom date's name?

MADELINE. Wait, it was something gorgeous.

MATT. Patricia Tatenhoff.

MADELINE. Rolls off the tongue!

MATT. Patty Tatts.

ERNESTINE. Be nice.

MATT. Whatever happened to that handsome specimen of a woman?

BILLY. She drowned her three babies.

ERNESTINE & MADELINE.	**MATT.**
Really?	I saw it in her eyes.

BILLY. No.

Maybe, I just said that to shut you guys up.

She ended up having sex with Rory Brogan in the handicapped bathroom.

MADELINE. Rory 'the clap' Brogan?!

BILLY. It was one of the worst nights of my life.

MATT. Sounds like it was worse for Patty Tatts.

The clap is forever.

MADELINE. Ewww.

BILLY. Joan.

I'm dating a girl named Joan.

ERNESTINE. Oh, goose, why didn't you say something?

MADELINE. Joan, that's such a plebian name.

ERNESTINE. When do we get to meet her?

MADELINE. Yeah, Billy, when do we get to meet her?

BILLY. If you get to meet her.

ERNESTINE. Are you worried we're going to embarrass you?

MADELINE. They will embarrass you.

MATT. It's a promise.

BILLY. I don't even know if she would call me her boyfriend.

ERNESTINE. But she might.

BILLY. She might.

ERNESTINE. Oh, goose, this is fantastic news.

BILLY. Are we done with the interrogation now?

ERNESTINE. We want to catch up with you two, we don't see you.

MADELINE. Because we don't live here.

BILLY. We've established this.

I'm going out.

MADELINE. I'm coming.

MATT. Count me in, too.

ERNESTINE. Wait.

For one moment.

To pause, to stake a claim.

To say we will have this hour, we will notice all we have.

(**JOAN** *enters carrying a wrapped present.*)

(**JOAN** *is nervous. She's always nervous.*)

JOAN. I didn't know what color nail polish would reflect your interior life.

BILLY. That's giving away what the present is, Joan.

JOAN. Damn you, Joan.

I apologize, I'm not accustomed to charged social situations and am also a stranger to my own heart!

(**ERNESTINE** *opens the present, pretends to be surprised.*)

ERNESTINE. Nail polish!

JOAN. My mother and I used to paint our nails every year.

And since you adore rituals and because she died suddenly during a parade I thought we could continue the tradition together.

(**ERNESTINE** *reads the colors of the nail polish.*)

ERNESTINE. That's so thoughtful.

'Gobsmacked.'

'Hurlyburly.'

'Finish Me Off.'

JOAN. Finish Me Off is my favorite, and necessary on occasion.

MADELINE. Ewww.

(**MATT** *and* **MADELINE** *try not to laugh but can't help themselves.*)

JOAN. And I now realize an awkward thing to say in front of you, I am filled with shame.

BILLY. Don't be, honey.

ERNESTINE. You two coming all this way, that's my real gift.

We're so happy to finally meet you.

JOAN. I'm so happy to be invited!

William has told me so much about what your birthday cake means to you.

Made of, 'Stardust and atoms left over from creation.'

ERNESTINE. I didn't know he was listening.

MADELINE. We pretty much had to memorize the entire speech.

BILLY. Since we were kids.

MADELINE. Eggs, butter, sugar, salt.

BILLY. The humblest ingredients.

MADELINE, BILLY & MATT. Look deeper and you'll find the story of the universe.

ERNESTINE. I'm glad I provided you all with some amusement.

JOAN. And finally I get to meet the legendary *(Mispronounced.)* Atman.

BILLY. *(Correcting.)* Atman.

JOAN. The legendary Atman.

'The divinity within myself.

Within all our selves.'

Namaste.

> *(***JOAN*** bows but knocks cake ingredients over.)*

Agggghhhhh!!!!

> *(***JOAN*** attempts to pick up the mess with little degree of success.)*

You ruin everything, Joan, They're all laughing at you.

BILLY. Nobody's laughing at you.

MADELINE. I kind of am.

ERNESTINE. We are not laughing.

JOAN. They're being polite, Joan, stop saying your name, Joan Joan Joan...

> *(***JOAN*** battles her mind with little degree of success.)*

I think I need a few minutes alone.

MADELINE. I agree.

BILLY. Enough!

ERNESTINE. Take your time, Joan, There's no rush. We are so happy to finally meet you.

> (**JOAN** *curtsies and in another lost battle with her mind blurts out in an odd British accent:*)

JOAN. Fare thee well, ma lady.

BILLY. Second door on the left.

JOAN. My left or your left?

BILLY. They're the same honey.

JOAN. What is happening????

> (**JOAN** *goes.*)

BILLY. She's nervous.

MATT. No shit.

BILLY. We're getting married.

MADELINE. Wow.

MATT. Wow.

ERNESTINE. Wow! We're so happy!

BILLY. So if you don't like her I don't care, keep it to yourself.

MADELINE. William, so assertive.

BILLY. I liked you better when I thought cynicism and a general lack of goodwill were charming.

MADELINE. Don't break my heart.

ERNESTINE. Stop.

Billy.

Our family includes everyone you choose to bring into this house, so please tell Joan she's a welcome addition to our life.

Right?

MATT. Right.

Absolutely.

A very welcome addition.

BILLY. I'm going to go check on here.

ERNESTINE. Tell her I would love to paint our nails together whenever she's ready.

MADELINE. And maybe give her some of my valium.

BILLY. Go play in traffic.

MADELINE. They're in the bottom drawer of the bathroom.

(**BILLY** *goes.*)

ERNESTINE. Married.

MATT. Married.

ERNESTINE. A second ago I washed him in this sink.

In this sink.

MATT. Five minutes ago we watched him take his first steps right here.

ERNESTINE. Married.

MATT. Married.

MADELINE. Do we have time to shoot some hoops before the party?

MATT. Ernestine?

ERNESTINE. A quick game.

MADELINE. You're so done.

MATT. Big talker over here.

MADELINE. I'm serious, I'll break your spirit.

MATT. We'll see.

> (**MATT** *and* **MADELINE** *exit.*)

> (**ERNESTINE** *is alone.*)

ERNESTINE. So quickly.

Like a breath.

> (**JOAN** *enters holding a baby.*)

> (*She is not the most maternal person in the world.*)

JOAN. Please please please please stop crying.

ERNESTINE. Let me.

> (**ERNESTINE** *takes the baby.*)

Hello, beautiful. Let me look at you.

JOAN. You have a gift.

ERNESTINE. Lots of practice.

Thank you for coming all this way on my birthday, Alexandra.

You are the greatest present I could possibly imagine.

> (*The baby quiets.*)

JOAN. Some people have children and say, 'now I understand what life is about.'

Me?

Not so much.

Most of my day is spent praying she'll go to sleep and the rest is wondering what my life would be like if I hadn't had her.

I have, as you know, remained a stranger to my own heart.

I'm so tired.

ERNESTINE. Sit, Joanie.

Rest.

>   (**BILLY** *plays piano in the other room.*)

>   (*He's gotten much better.*)

Listen, Alexandra.

Your father used to be one of the worst musicians in the world.

>   (*They listen to the piano.*)

>   (*Really listen.*)

>   (**MATT** *enters.*)

MATT. He got better.

ERNESTINE. I told you.

MATT. May I?

>   (**MATT** *takes* **ALEX.***)

>   (*Coos to her.*)

>   (*He's a good grandfather.*)

>   (**ERNESTINE** *and* **JOAN** *both watch.*)

Hey, Alley.

MATT. It might be a little early to get into this, but in terms of romance, kites and strings go together.

Your grandmother is my kite.

And I am her string.

>   (**MATT** *kisses* **ERNESTINE.**)

JOAN. Even He's more maternal than I am.

MATT. Happy birthday.

ERNESTINE. Thank you, Matt.

MATT. Where are we with the cake?

ERNESTINE. Still on the batter.

MATT. I'll have her back in time for the party.

Every year we make the same cake, Alley.

Someday you'll get to do it, too.

>   *(He goes.)*

ERNESTINE. What colors do we have this year?

JOAN. 'Life is a Cabaret' or 'Bang the Dream'

JOAN. 'Plum Seduction' or 'Oops Not There, Senator'

JOAN. Pink or neutral?

ERNESTINE & JOAN. Neutral.

JOAN. I thought it was time to embrace simplicity.

>   (**JOAN** *paints* **ERNESTINE**'s *nails.*)

ERNESTINE. Painting our nails has become so special to me, Joanie, I look forward to it every year.

I know it's what you used to do with your own mother.

I'm so happy you decided to share it with me.

JOAN. I tried to make your cake last year for William's birthday.

ERNESTINE. How did it go?

JOAN. Stardust and the machinery of the cosmos?

Not so much.

A sad mess more unholy than the Jell-O casserole that killed my cousin.

ERNESTINE. You've got to be easier on yourself.

Breathe.

    (**JOAN** *breathes.*)

    (**JOAN** *looks out the window.*)

JOAN. Alex don't climb on that!

ERNESTINE. Breathe, Joanie.

JOAN. My life is spent crippled by graphic visions in which she gets killed or kidnapped or both or worse.

Does the crushing anxiety ever go away?

ERNESTINE. Never.

It becomes part of you.

And soon you won't be able to remember yourself without it.

    (*The piano music in the next room finishes.**)

    (**BILLY** *enters.*)

    (**ERNESTINE** *and* **JOAN** *applaud,* **BILLY** *bows.*)

---

* A license to produce BIRTHDAY CANDLES does not include a performance license for any third-party or copyrighted music. Licensees should create an original composition or use music in the public domain. For further information, please see Music Use Note on page 3.

ERNESTINE AND JOAN. Bravo, bravo.

> (**JOAN** *has rehearsed this joke:*)

JOAN. A tourist asks a New Yorker, 'how do I get to Carnegie Hall?'

And he says take the R train to 57th and you'll see it across 7th Avenue, you can't miss it.

BILLY. I think the punchline is 'Practice practice practice.'

JOAN. Which is much funnier, and inspiring.

> (**BILLY** *gives* **ERNESTINE** *her present.*)

BILLY. Happy birthday.

JOAN. Do you enjoy champagne?

Damn you, Joan.

> (**ERNESTINE** *opens it.*)

> (*Pretends to be surprised.*)

ERNESTINE. Champagne!

This is a first.

BILLY. Dad!

MATT. (*Offstage.*) What???

BILLY. Come in here!!

MATT. (*Offstage.*) I don't want to!

BILLY. Please!

JOAN. Alex!!!

Don't get killed or kidnapped for five minutes please!!!!

> (**MATT** *enters.*)

MATT. Where are we with the cake?

ERNESTINE. I haven't even put it in yet.

BILLY. Mom.

Dad.

We wanted to discuss something with you.

MATT. I don't like the sound of this.

ERNESTINE. Be nice.

BILLY. An investment.

JOAN. An opportunity!

MATT. 'Get in at the ground floor'.

'You'd be a fool not to jump at the chance.'

ERNESTINE. Go ahead, Billy.

BILLY. Two words.

Real estate.

MATT. I agree, those are two words.

ERNESTINE. Let's hear them out.

BILLY. Please don't undermine me.

MATT. Who's undermining you?

BILLY. You always told me to take the initiative.

This is me taking the initiative!

MATT. Begging for money is not taking the initiative.

BILLY. That is undermining.

JOAN. Stand back, Joan, You've got this.

> (**JOAN** *has endlessly rehearsed her sales pitch.*)

What is paper currency?

JOAN. A promissory note, people think of it as something tangible?

Ladies and gentlemen it's representative.

Ground.

Earth.

Now, that is an asset that doesn't go away.

MATT. First an entrepreneur, then a mortgage broker.

Now what?

A land baron?

BILLY. This is different!

MATT. You can't sustain anything!

You don't understand commitment!

ERNESTINE. We're together so little, can we not fight for one day, please?

BILLY. Tell him, He's the one attacking me.

MATT. Attacking? What, we're in a war all of a sudden?

BILLY. You told me to take the initiative!

MATT. Do you think I enjoyed going to work every day?

BILLY. I know what commitment is.

MATT. A man provides for his family.

BILLY. So now you're a hero, is that it?

MATT. The world doesn't owe you free dinner.

BILLY. What does that even mean???

MATT. Grow up!

BILLY. I am grown up!

ERNESTINE. Stop!!!!!!

(They stop.)

A rest.

Please.

To notice what we have left.

(A tiny rest.)

*(**MADELINE** enters.)*

MADELINE. Is it time for the party yet?

ERNESTINE. Athena, you're awake.

MADELINE. I don't have a name anymore. I'm anonymous.

BILLY. What?

How?

MATT. A redefinition?

MADELINE. I don't have a definition anymore, either.

There aren't any.

In me.

Or in the world.

We can name it whatever we like but it's all random, there are no patterns anywhere.

ERNESTINE. Why don't you get some rest, we'll come get you when it's time for the party.

MADELINE. Rest!

Rest!

That's all I do!

MATT. You need it, Maddy.

MADELINE. I need to see the pattern!!

Who dies, who lives, why?

MADELINE. Billy finds a nervous girl, your marriage grows tired, my mind breaks.

Why?

Where is it written?

Was it true before I was born?

Fate?

Or do I have some agency in the scenes of my life?

MATT. Slow down Maddy. Slow down.

ERNESTINE. Did you take your medication today?

MADELINE. Really?

We're going to do this in front of Joan?

JOAN. I'm part of this family, too.

MADELINE. The extraneous part, the part that can be excised without loss.

BILLY. Don't talk to my wife that way.

MADELINE. Like tonsils or wisdom teeth.

JOAN. I don't like you.

Joan you spoke your truth.

MADELINE. I'm going out.

ERNESTINE. But my party.

MADELINE. Time is a lie, the party already happened, it went great.

MATT. Maddy, can we ask where you're going?

MADELINE. You can ask but there is no answer.

There are none.

In me, or you or anywhere.

(**MADELINE** *goes.*)

MATT. Maddy!

BILLY. She's twenty seven, living back at home, and you make me feel ashamed to borrow money.

MATT. She's sick!

You're a pussy. Big difference.

Hey, Maddy, wait up.

(**MATT** *goes.*)

BILLY. Joan.

Let's pack our things, we're leaving.

ERNESTINE. I don't see you.

JOAN. Alex!!!!

Very carefully climb down from there, we're leaving!!!

(**JOAN** *goes.*)

ERNESTINE. I don't get any time with my granddaughter.

My birthday.

It's the only time we're all together.

BILLY. I can't do this anymore.

ERNESTINE. Stay.

(*He goes.*)

(**ERNESTINE** *is alone.*)

(**MADELINE** *enters.*)

MADELINE. Is it time for the party yet?

ERNESTINE. Not quite yet, darling.

MADELINE. Hey, what's up, Atman.

Three.

MADELINE. Two.

One.

Boom.

The world anew.

Wouldn't that be amazing?

If I could erase everything, my name, my facts, and create them again.

ERNESTINE. That's what you have here at home, a second chance.

MADELINE. Maybe this is just a rehearsal.

Maybe I am just pretending to be a daughter, a sister, pretending to have opinions, friends, pretending that I'm sick.

ERNESTINE. You're not pretending.

MADELINE. I've always waited for someone to take me into another room and tell me when the real show was going to start.

ERNESTINE. It's now. It's real.

MADELINE. Time for measurements.

ERNESTINE. Not this year.

MADELINE. Every year.

Every year.

> (**MADELINE** *pushes* **ERNESTINE** *up against the wall.*)

Shoes.

> (**MADELINE** *bends down and takes* **ERNESTINE**'s *shoes off herself.*)

Thank you for being my Mom.

ERNESTINE. Stay.

MADELINE. I can't.

ERNESTINE. Please.

> (**MADELINE** *steps out of the play.*)

> (**MATT** *enters.*)
>
> (*They bake the cake together.*)
>
> (*Silence.*)
>
> (*He breaks down and cries and walks off.*)
>
> (**ERNESTINE** *is alone.*)

> (**KENNETH** *enters.*)
>
> (*Same as the first time.*)
>
> (*He attempts to get her to notice him without scaring her.*)
>
> (*It doesn't work.*)

ERNESTINE. Aggghhh!

KENNETH. Agghhhh!!!

ERNESTINE. A fifty year old man and you can't make an entrance.

KENNETH. I'm still practicing.

> (**KENNETH** *has a present that is obviously a telescope.*)

Happy birthday.

It's a sweater.

ERNESTINE. I don't need a telescope, Kenneth.

KENNETH. Who does?

ERNESTINE. Astronomers.

KENNETH. And creepers.

ERNESTINE & KENNETH. Ewwwwwww.

KENNETH. You've always talked about your pilgrimage toward finding your place in the scale of the universe.

This will help.

Very literally.

ERNESTINE. That's very thoughtful. Thank you, Kenneth.

KENNETH. Those of us that believe in the multiverse think that some radiation in space is leftover starlight from a future universe.

Future because in the physical laws of that universe, time flows in the opposite direction. Trippy right? I thought about it all last night until I forgot my name.

ERNESTINE. Madeline has been dead for almost three years.

My mother over thirty.

KENNETH. I can still see them standing right there.

ERNESTINE. The pattern keeps getting stranger, Kenneth.

Between the living and the dead.

KENNETH. Exponentially stranger every year.

ERNESTINE. 'If there's anything I can do.'

KENNETH. Yeah, there is.

Bring them back.

ERNESTINE. Bring them all back.

KENNETH. In addition to the telescope, I bear the gift of pin the tail on the donkey.

(He takes out pin the tail on the donkey.)

ERNESTINE. No.

KENNETH. Yes.

ERNESTINE. That is the world's stupidest game.

KENNETH. I agree.

But it's fun.

You remember what having fun is like?

ERNESTINE. Not lately.

KENNETH. Allow me to remind you.

As I'm attaching this, I'm noticing this year's donkey has longer eyelashes, and she has more of a 'come hither' look.

*(**KENNETH** checks in on Atman.)*

How's Atman the 43rd?

ERNESTINE. Atman the 46th.

KENNETH. Three in one year?

ERNESTINE. Don't start.

KENNETH. You beast.

ERNESTINE. It's been a rough time in the goldfish world.

KENNETH. Hello, Atman the 46th.

I'm Kenneth, no, no, please, don't get up.

You don't remember me because you are removed from the causal plane of existence and live in a place of stillness, quietly watching the drama of the world unfold.

Three, two, one, boom.

Best seat in the house.

ERNESTINE. How's Doris?

KENNETH. Gone.

ERNESTINE. Business?

KENNETH. Divorce.

ERNESTINE. Kenneth.

KENNETH. Not even a trial separation or regular separation,

Which I sort of prefer, I'm more of a rip the band aid off fast kinda fella.

ERNESTINE. Did she tell you why?

KENNETH. She sure did.

(He searches in his pocket.)

(Finds the note.)

Let's see. 'Hi Ken.' She still calls me Ken. 'I don't love you or respect you. Bye. Doris.'

ERNESTINE. Kenneth, I'm so sorry.

(He flips the note over.)

KENNETH. Wait for it. 'PS, I never loved you or respected you. I only married you out of an equal measure of obligation and pity.'

(He carefully folds it back up and puts it in his pocket.)

ERNESTINE. Ouch.

KENNETH. Right? The PS was a bit gauche for my taste.

ERNESTINE. Completely.

KENNETH. Like, I get it already.

ERNESTINE. Maybe it's a blessing in disguise.

KENNETH. For once in my life I would appreciate a blessing out of disguise.

ERNESTINE. How are you doing?

KENNETH. Probably I'm in denial and the full weight of being fifty and abjectly alone forever will sink in, but until then, top of the pops, I feel free.

ERNESTINE. Free.

Oh God, what I wouldn't give.

There are so many places I want to see.

The Boulevard St. Germain in Paris.

Bora Bora.

Do you love the ocean?

KENNETH. I'm scared of the shower.

ERNESTINE. How long have we known each other, Kenneth?

KENNETH. We practiced kissing in your backyard when we were seven but I wasn't practicing so forty three years.

ERNESTINE. Have we changed?

KENNETH. Of course we have.

Weariness? Sure.

Regrets. More than necessary.

Wisdom? Still waiting.

ERNESTINE. How did those two kids become us?

KENNETH. *(As Queen Lear.)* 'So we'll live

And pray, and sing, and tell old tales

And laugh

At gilded butterflies, and hear poor rogues

Talk of court news, and we'll talk with them, too.'

ERNESTINE. You're getting better.

KENNETH. That means a lot coming from you, I mean, people still talk about your triumphant performance as Queen Lear.

ERNESTINE. No, they don't.

KENNETH. I do.

People politely listen.

Will you finish it?

ERNESTINE. Kenneth.

KENNETH. Please.

(Watch out, she's even better than last time.)

ERNESTINE. *(As Queen Lear.)* 'So we'll live

And pray, and sing, and tell old tales

And laugh

At gilded butterflies, and hear poor rogues

Talk of court news, and we'll talk with them, too

Who loses and who wins

Who's in, who's out

And take upon the mystery of things

As if we were God's spies.'

*(**KENNETH** applauds, she curtsies.)*

KENNETH. Like a fine wine.

ERNESTINE. Closer to the end than the beginning.

KENNETH. Way closer for me, I drink too much, I quit smoking like twenty minutes ago, and I'm up most nights wracked with anxiety, regret, and shame.

ERNESTINE. I went to the department store to pick out a new scarf.

And I couldn't.

Thirty minutes, staring, walking through the aisles.

A clerk actually came up to me and asked if anything was wrong.

I'm fifty years old and I can't pick out a scarf for myself!

KENNETH. I'm in love with you.

ERNESTINE. What?

KENNETH. What?

ERNESTINE. You're in love with me?

KENNETH. You really didn't know.

ERNESTINE. No, how could I?

KENNETH. How could you not?

I come around here like a puppy.

Every excuse. The stupidest questions.

Is this the proper use of a semicolon?

Should I run for congress?

ERNESTINE. This is a knee jerk reaction.

A divorce is a trauma.

KENNETH. No.

Since I could feel, that's how long I've loved you.

ERNESTINE. Kenneth, I don't feel the same way.

(Long pause.)

KENNETH. Yet.

ERNESTINE. Ever.

KENNETH. Hope.

ERNESTINE. Insanity.

> *(He kisses her.)*

KENNETH. Hope.

> *(**MATT** enters.)*

MATT. Sorry I'm late.

ERNESTINE. You're right on time honey.

MATT. Hiya, Kenny.

KENNETH. Kenneth.

MATT. Kenny.

KENNETH. Asshole.

MATT. Look out, big talker over here.

ERNESTINE. Okay boys, enough.

We'll see you at the party Kenneth.

KENNETH. I'll see you in forty seven minutes. Forty six minutes and fifty nine seconds, fifty eight seconds, fifty seven...

> *(He goes.)*

MATT. Kenny jumped the gun on the party again, huh?

ERNESTINE. Doris left him.

MATT. I'm shocked it took this long.

ERNESTINE. Don't be cruel.

MATT. Cruel?

The man lusts after my wife.

Regular neighbors ask to borrow a cup of sugar.

Kenny asks how to correctly use punctuation.

Happy birthday.

(A present.)

ERNESTINE. You didn't have to.

MATT. I sorta did.

What kind of husband doesn't give his wife a present on her fiftieth birthday?

ERNESTINE. A bottle of perfume.

ERNESTINE. A bottle of perfume.

ERNESTINE. A bottle of perfume.

Are you having an affair?

MATT. What?

Why would you ask me that?

> (**ERNESTINE** *takes out a condom and puts it on the counter.*)

ERNESTINE. It's a condom.

MATT. I was holding onto that for a friend.

ERNESTINE. Late nights at the office.

Sudden business trips.

You're not a spy.

Tell me the truth and I won't be mad.

MATT. Can we have a nice birthday?

Where are we with the cake?

ERNESTINE. You feel guilt?

This is the opportunity to absolve yourself.

Say the words and I promise you'll feel better immediately.

MATT. I'm having an affair.

ERNESTINE. You're a pig.

MATT. You said you wouldn't be mad!

ERNESTINE. I was lying!

With who?

MATT. Donna Kaplan.

ERNESTINE. My best friend from high school?

MATT. She was your best friend, I don't think you were her best friend.

ERNESTINE. How long?

MATT. Three years.

ERNESTINE. You look me in the eyes for three years and say you love me?

MATT. Because I do.

ERNESTINE. Get out of my house!

MATT. I wanted to tell you.

ERNESTINE. You're a coward.

MATT. Our marriage has become an arrangement. You know this, too.

You're quietly dying, too.

ERNESTINE. A rebel against the universe and this is what I've become.

MATT. It started after Maddy died.

You and I, we weren't talking

We barely saw each other, let alone slept together, I tried, I got tired of trying.

ERNESTINE. So it's my fault?

MATT. Maybe this is a good thing.

This is me.

This is honest.

ERNESTINE. Honest?

How much honesty do I get?

I chose you every day.

> (**ERNESTINE** *calmly takes the blue ribbon out of her hair.*)

> (*Gives it back to* **MATT.**)

MATT. I made a mistake!

ERNESTINE. I'm going to kiss you now and then we're finished.

MATT. An affair.

ERNESTINE. A breaking.

MATT. Ernestine, honey.

ERNESTINE. I gave you all my best hours.

> (*She kisses him.*)

> (*She turns back to the cake.*)

MATT. Hey.

Hey, Ernestine, come on.

A thirty-five-year marriage.

We are going to break up like this?

Talk to me.

> (*She's not going to talk to him.*)

This is on you.

MATT. You remember that.

> *(He is about to say about a million things but says none of them and instead exits.)*

> (**ERNESTINE** *was able to hold it together long enough for him to leave the room but now she allows herself to cry.)*

> (**ERNESTINE** *alone.)*

> *(No one in the house this year.)*

ERNESTINE. Just the two of us this year, Atman.

> (**ERNESTINE** *puts the cake into the oven.)*

It's a new world for me, too.

> *(It's not sad.)*

> *(It's still.)*

> *(With no one coming to the party, she sits, she waits silently for her cake to be ready.)*

> *(Piano music rises from the next room.*)*

> *(By now* **BILLY** *has gotten really good.)*

> (**ERNESTINE** *stops.)*

> *(She listens.)*

> *(Really listens.)*

> (**ALEX** *enters. Seventeen.)*

---

* A license to produce BIRTHDAY CANDLES does not include a performance license for any third-party or copyrighted music. Licensees should create an original composition or use music in the public domain. For further information, please see Music Use Note on page 3.

ALEX. Grandma, have I wasted my life?

ERNESTINE. You're seventeen.

ALEX. In the career of my soul, how many times have I turned from wonder?

ERNESTINE. Listen Alexandra.

Your father used to be one of the worst musicians in the world.

(They listen.)

What colors this year?

ALEX. 'Finish Me Off Again.'

'Yes, Right There, Madame Secretary'

'Neutral.'

ERNESTINE & ALEX. Neutral.

*(***ALEX*** paints her nails.)*

ALEX. My first memory was right here.

At your knees, making this cake with you.

ERNESTINE. You never told me.

ALEX. Tasting the batter before you put it in the oven.

'If you look deeper, Alexandra, you'll find the story of the universe.'

ERNESTINE. You were listening.

ALEX. I tried to look.

Maybe other people saw the story.

Me?

Not so much.

No story, no pattern, just chaos.

ALEX. Is it my fault my parents broke up?

ERNESTINE. No.

Never think that.

ALEX. I said, okay, Alex, you can keep everyone together if you knuckle up and fight for it.

I fought but I wasn't strong enough.

ERNESTINE. Stop.

No one is.

Not you or me or anyone.

Despite our greatest hopes, we can't make anyone stay.

*(The music ends and **BILLY** enters.)*

Bravo, bravo!

*(**BILLY** bows with a flourish.)*

BILLY & ERNESTINE. Practice, practice, practice.

BILLY. We'd better be going.

Alex, get your things.

ALEX. Ten minutes.

BILLY. This is not a negotiation, young lady. Get your things.

ALEX. You're a shadow in a suit posing as a human, you should be ashamed of yourself.

*(**ALEX** goes.)*

ERNESTINE. Don't take it personally.

BILLY. Was I ever so young, so self-involved?

ERNESTINE. To the letter.

BILLY. I apologize, retroactively.

ERNESTINE. Accepted.

BILLY. Can we talk about Christmas?

We'll fly in on that Thursday, I have a conference in Arizona, so when Alex goes to Joan's, I'll fly out the same day.

ERNESTINE. How are you holding up, goose?

BILLY. You don't have to worry about me.

ERNESTINE. You've put on weight.

BILLY. Thank you for noticing.

ERNESTINE. People eat a lot during a divorce.

Aunt Lucy looked like she swallowed a buffet.

BILLY. You never gained any weight during yours.

ERNESTINE. Thank you for noticing.

BILLY. How are you?

ERNESTINE. I'm amazing.

BILLY. Because you look amazing.

ERNESTINE. I do?

BILLY. You kind of glow.

ERNESTINE. A personal renaissance.

BILLY. Any specific reason?

ERNESTINE. I started a business.

BILLY. Get out of here.

ERNESTINE. I'm serious!

Ernestine's Just Desserts.

BILLY. Mom.

ERNESTINE. CEO, founder, lone employee.

BILLY. This is fantastic.

ERNESTINE. Small.

I sell to three bakeries.

BILLY. I can't think of better news.

ERNESTINE. It keeps me occupied.

Important.

For the mind.

When the house got so empty.

I didn't know who I was if I wasn't taking care of someone.

So I decided to find out.

ERNESTINE. I'll be gone for ten months.

This is a copy of my itinerary if you'd like to keep track of my whereabouts.

BILLY. You're sure you're going to be okay alone?

ERNESTINE. Okay?

I'm going to be ecstatically alone.

BILLY. Take so many pictures, keep track of every day so when you come home you can tell me the story.

(**ERNESTINE** *has a photo album.*)

ERNESTINE. There I am sauntering down the Boulevard St. Germain in Paris. It's true, they really are incredibly rude to Americans.

There I am with my sherpa at the base camp of Mr. Everest.

BILLY. Who's that?

ERNESTINE. My lascivious tango instructor in Buenos Aires.

So forward.

I didn't mind.

BILLY. I wish I could have gone with you.

ERNESTINE. I don't.

I had to go on this trip alone.

> (**MATT** *enters.*)

> (*He looks tired, hollowed.*)

MATT. Hello Ernestine.

ERNESTINE. Matt.

BILLY. Dad?

MATT. Hello, Billy.

ERNESTINE. What are you doing here?

> (**ALEX** *enters.*)

ALEX. Surprise!

I invited Grandpa.

So we could celebrate your birthday as a family again.

MATT. Where are we with the cake?

BILLY. Alex, what were you thinking?

MATT. I can help.

ALEX. What?

BILLY. You know damn well what.

ALEX. Kites and strings go together.

MATT. I still know every step.

BILLY. Sabotaging your grandmother's birthday like this.

ALEX. This is our family.

ALEX. Happy?

No.

But let's admit that truth and move forward.

This is who we are, this is honest.

MATT. Which is what I've saying since the beginning.

BILLY. Mom's been herself since you left.

And on her birthday you do this, how dare you?

>   (**KENNETH** *enters carrying balloons.*)
>
>   (*Surveys the situation.*)

KENNETH. Holy shit.

>   (**KENNETH** *goes.*)

MATT. Have I made mistakes?

I'm the first to admit that.

ALEX. Forgiveness.

The heart of most major religions.

BILLY. You broke this family.

Breathe one second of authenticity.

Walk away.

ERNESTINE. Time for measurements.

BILLY. Not this year.

ERNESTINE. Every year.

>   (**ERNESTINE** *measures herself.*)
>
>   (*Writes on the wall.*)
>
>   (*Everyone is silenced.*)

Ernestine.

Age seventy.

The decline has begun.

Almost nothing left to notice. That's honest.

(They're together for just one second.)

BILLY. I love you mom, I'll call you when we land.

Alex, we're leaving.

*(***BILLY*** goes.)*

ALEX. You okay the rest of the way, Grandpa?

*(***ALEX*** hugs **MATT**.)*

MATT. Thanks, Alley, I'll take it from here.

*(***ALEX*** hugs **ERNESTINE**.)*

ALEX. Give him a chance.

Forgiveness.

The heart of most major religions.

Namaste, Atman.

*(***ALEX*** goes.)*

ERNESTINE. On my birthday.

MATT. You're the only person who knows me.

I'm only asking for company.

I should have called, I shouldn't have made such a dramatic entrance, that's on me.

But it would be a pity for my traveling companion through this life to know nothing of me anymore.

(Silence.)

MATT. I was at the bakery the other day.

'Ernestine's Just Desserts.'

It's everywhere.

I couldn't believe it.

ERNESTINE. You couldn't believe I could have my own business, thank you.

MATT. No, I couldn't believe how much I missed it.

This.

The smell.

The flour.

I had every chance for happiness.

Right here.

And I'm not asking for it back.

ERNESTINE. Good, because that would make you an insane person.

MATT. Only to spend a little time.

Every once in a while. You're my kite. I'm your string.

ERNESTINE. What would we have done, Matt?

If someone could have told us this is how we'd end up?

MATT. It doesn't have to be the end.

ERNESTINE. This kitchen.

My eighteenth birthday.

A brave speech.

You touched my hand.

What would we have done?

MATT. I would ask to do it all over again.

We raised a family, Ernestine.

A beautiful family.

> *(**MATT** sits.)*
>
> *(Two years later.)*
>
> *(He's had a stroke, he can't speak.)*
>
> *(**ERNESTINE** feeds **MATT** with a spoon.)*
>
> *(Drool, she wipes it up.)*

ERNESTINE. They say we travel childhood to childhood.

Who knew it would be so literal?

Feeding a broken man baby food.

The same food I fed our own children.

> *(He has a present sitting next to him.)*
>
> *(**MATT** speaks with difficulty.)*

MATT. Happy birthday.

> *(It's her blue ribbon, that he gave her when they were eighteen.)*
>
> *(She puts it in her hair.)*

ERNESTINE. A blue ribbon.

And?

MATT. Still stunning.

> *(She sits. **ERNESTINE** holds his hand.)*

ERNESTINE. Just a little longer until we're ready with the cake.

Okay?

(Silence.)

(**MATT** *stands up. Steps out of time, out of the play.)*

(**ALEX** *enters carrying her baby.)*

ALEX. Please please please please stop crying.

ERNESTINE. Let me, Alex.

(**ERNESTINE** *takes the baby.)*

Hi, beautiful. Just let me look at you, Ernestine.

I still can't get over that you named her after me.

ALEX. It's a beautiful name, I thought it should be put to more use.

ERNESTINE. Thank you for coming all this way, Ernestine.

You are the greatest present I could possibly imagine.

ALEX. Some people have children and say, 'Now I understand what life is about.'

I am now one of those people.

ERNESTINE. You met your heart.

ALEX. I'm pregnant again.

ERNESTINE. A blessing out of disguise.

(Piano music.)

ALEX. A boy. I'm going to name him after my Dad.

Do you think he'll be happy?

ERNESTINE. I think he'll be ecstatic.

BILLY. *(Offstage.)* Are you two coming?

ALEX. It's time for the party, Grandma.

ERNESTINE. Can I have a second with Ernestine first?

ALEX. One second, you will not spend half the party cleaning up again, young lady.

ERNESTINE. I promise I'll be right behind you.

>*(She's gone.)*

Look, Ernestine.

That's the moon.

So much of the world's asleep, but here.

It's time for my party.

Will you come celebrate it with me?

I always had a million things to do.

And when I looked up?

Everyone was already gone.

>*(**ERNIE** and **WILLIAM** enter, practicing their audition for Queen Lear.)*

>*(A thirteen year old **WILLIAM** enters grandly followed by a fifteen year old **ERNIE**.)*

WILLIAM. *(As Cordello.)* 'Unhappy that I am, I cannot heave

My heart into my mouth.

I love your majesty

According to my bond; no more no less'

ERNIE. *(As Queen Lear.)* 'How, now, Cordello! Mend your speech a little,

Lest it may mar your fortunes.'

WILLIAM. Are you really going to do it like that?

ERNIE. No good?

WILLIAM. You are at a nine when I need you at a two.

ERNESTINE. The high school is reviving Queen Lear?

WILLIAM. A third wave feminist interpretation.

ERNESTINE. I played the tragic queen myself to minor acclaim.

(**ALEX** *enters.*)

ALEX. William, Ernestine, come help me set up the piñata.

ERNIE. Five minutes, mom.

WILLIAM. Ten minutes, mom.

ALEX. This is not a negotiation, come help me set up the piñata.

WILLIAM. You are a shadow in –

ALEX. – don't start with that, I'm serious.

(**ALEX** *goes.*)

(**ERNESTINE** *gives* **ERNIE** *the baby she was holding.*)

(*It's a doll.*)

ERNIE. Oh God where did you find my doll she was my favorite toy ever.

ERNESTINE. She was my daughter's favorite too.

It's been almost forty years since Madeline died and I still miss her so much. I don't have words to say how much I miss her.

ERNIE. Wherever Madeline is I know she misses you just as much.

WILLIAM. Come on, Teney, It's time.

ERNESTINE. Just let me look at you William.

Just for one second, Ernestine, let me look.

(For one second she looks.)

You two go ahead now.

ERNIE. You will not spend half the party cleaning up again, young lady.

ERNESTINE. I'll be right behind.

I promise.

(As **WILLIAM** *and* **ERNIE** *go:)*

ERNIE. I'm totally going to break the piñata before you.

WILLIAM. Look out, big talker over here.

ERNIE. I'll break your spirit.

WILLIAM. We'll see.

(They're gone.)

*(***ERNESTINE** *cleans up.)*

*(***KENNETH** *enters.)*

(Same as the first time.)

(He tries to get her attention without scaring her.)

ERNESTINE. Aggghhh!

KENNETH. Agghhhh!!!

ERNESTINE. You've got to stop doing that!!!

KENNETH. I'm sorry!!!

ERNESTINE. It's been eight decades, Kenneth, You've had more than enough practice!

KENNETH. I'll do better next time!

I promise.

ERNESTINE. Hi.

KENNETH. Hi.

> *(They kiss.)*

Do they know?

ERNESTINE. Not yet.

KENNETH. You're ashamed of me.

ERNESTINE. Shut up.

KENNETH. What will people think?

ERNESTINE. Who cares?

We're eighty eight years old.

KENNETH. Happy birthday, sweetheart.

> *(A present, obviously not a sweater.)*

ERNESTINE. A sweater.

KENNETH. Nailed it.

> *(Opens it.)*

> *(A corsage.)*

ERNESTINE. A corsage.

KENNETH. Do you want to go to the prom with me?

ERNESTINE. Kenneth.

KENNETH. You said insanity.

ERNESTINE. You said hope.

KENNETH. I hate to say I told you so.

ERNESTINE. I've never been happier to be wrong about anything.

> *(He almost pins the corsage on her.)*

KENNETH. Could you?

ERNESTINE. Too sharp?

KENNETH. Hemophilia.

ERNESTINE. Let's not tempt fate at this point.

> *(She pins the corsage on herself.)*

KENNETH. And since I have to bring the prom to us.

> *(Another present.)*

> *(A radio.)*

I give you the gift of music.

> *(He turns it on with a flourish.)*

> *(A cha cha.)*

> *(***KENNETH*** *dances.)*

Can you handle this, little girl?

ERNESTINE. Watch yourself. I move like the sea moves.

KENNETH. Show me.

> *(***ERNESTINE*** *dances.)*

> *(She's amazing, not just based on her effort but because she moves like the sea moves.)*

> *(They dance, they fit together.)*

> *(They kiss.)*

I'm getting sea sick you're so beautiful.

> *(***BILLY*** *enters.)*

BILLY. No

BILLY. Fucking

Way.

ERNESTINE. Billy, we have something to tell you.

> *(Before they can say anything* **BILLY** *goes to* **KENNETH** *and hugs him hard.)*

BILLY. You are my hero.

KENNETH. That's a first.

BILLY. How long have you waited for her?

KENNETH. Since I could feel.

ERNESTINE. Kenneth.

> *(She kisses him.)*

KENNETH. Is it okay if I kiss your mom?

ERNESTINE. Don't ask permission.

KENNETH. Billy, I'm gonna kiss your mom.

> *(He dips her in a kiss.)*

(To **BILLY.***)* And now I want you to leave.

How was that?

ERNESTINE. Very assertive.

BILLY. Can I tell everyone?

KENNETH. If you don't, I'll send up a flare.

BILLY. Hey everybody, you're not going to believe this shit!

> *(***BILLY*** *goes.)*

KENNETH. In addition to the gift of music and a corsage.

Plane tickets.

Bora Bora.

ERNESTINE. You're scared of the shower.

KENNETH. But it's one of the world's top destinations for honeymooners.

>   *(A little box.)*

>   *(A ring.)*

>   *(Awwwwwww.)*

ERNESTINE. Yes.

KENNETH. Wait.

I have to do the knee thing first.

ERNESTINE. Your back.

KENNETH. Fuck it.

I've waited eight decades for this.

>   *(Ouch.)*

>   *(Getting down on one knee does hurt.)*

Ooof.

Probably call Dr. Shahibi tomorrow.

ERNESTINE. Sweetheart.

KENNETH. I have to.

ERNESTINE. You don't.

KENNETH. I have to.

ERNESTINE. Okay. You have to.

KENNETH. Ernestine Ashworth.

You told me again and again and again to stop loving you but I didn't listen because I'm built of heroic patience.

KENNETH. You are my best friend, pretty much my only friend, my love, my reason for being, my everything.

Will you be my wife?

(**ERNESTINE** *is crying.*)

ERNESTINE. Yes.

(*He slips on the ring.*)

You have to kiss me now, sweetheart.

KENNETH. Could you help me up first?

(*She does.*)

(*They kiss.*)

You are my witness, Atman the 71st.

ERNESTINE. Atman the 72nd.

KENNETH. When?

ERNESTINE. Two days ago.

KENNETH. You beast.

It's genocide by now.

ERNESTINE. Don't start.

KENNETH. You're a war criminal.

ERNESTINE. 'You are my witness...'

KENNETH. You are my witness, Atman the 72nd.

Whatever you are, whether it's the world's soul, the aspirational peace of existence, or the eternity that waits for each of us, thank you for waiting as long as I have for the love of my life to finally figure out that she loves me, too.

ERNESTINE. I'm sorry it took me so long, Kenneth.

KENNETH. Don't be. Victory tastes that much sweeter.

> *(He kisses her again.)*

> *(**ERNIE**, **WILLIAM** and **ALEX** enter.)*

ERNIE. No fucking way.

BILLY. I told you.

ALEX. You are my hero.

KENNETH. That's a second.

ERNESTINE. Kenneth asked me to marry him.

ERNIE. And?

KENNETH. Seriously?

How could anyone turn this action down?

ERNESTINE. I said yes.

> *(Screams from kids.)*

> *(**ALEX** gets champagne (the same bottle **JOAN** brought back in the day).)*

ALEX. Does everyone still enjoy champagne?

> *(Hoots and hollers from everyone regarding their love of champagne.)*

WILLIAM. Can I have some champagne, grandpa?

BILLY. I think it would be fine.

ALEX. Dad, He's thirteen.

BILLY. I think you should listen to your mother.

ERNIE. Kenneth, you bought such a beautiful ring.

KENNETH. Industry standard says three month's salary, but I decided on half my pension instead.

ERNESTINE. It's perfect, Kenneth.

KENNETH. You're perfect, sweetheart.

BILLY. A toast!

To the beautiful couple.

KENNETH. To the birthday girl.

Speech! Speech!

ALEX, ERNIE, WILLIAM, KENNETH & BILLY. Speech! Speech!

ERNESTINE. Oh, God, an audience.

> (**ERNESTINE** *may or may not indicate the audience, up to you.*)

The genius of a party is to offer us all a rest from the daily human errand to travel morning until night.

To stake a claim in an hour and say I will notice this.

The house full again, sounds of laughter and music, this hour shared with all of you is my favorite.

ALEX, ERNIE, WILLIAM, KENNETH & BILLY. Awwwwww.

> (**WILLIAM** *and* **ERNIE** *exit.*)

ALEX, KENNETH & BILLY. Speech! Speech!

ERNESTINE. The genius of a party is to offer us all a rest.

To stake a claim in an hour and say I will notice this.

But this hour shared with you three is my favorite.

KENNETH, BILLY & ALEX. Awwwww.

> (**ALEX** *and* **BILLY** *exit.*)

KENNETH. Speech! Speech!

ERNESTINE. I'm not giving a speech, sweetheart, It's just the two of us.

KENNETH. Then it's time for pin the tail on the donkey.

(**KENNETH** *ties a kitchen towel blindfold on her and spins her around.*)

ERNESTINE. This is the world's stupidest game.

KENNETH. You're right.

But it's fun.

You remember what fun is like?

ERNESTINE. I don't have to remember.

This is the most fun I've had in my entire life.

(*As* **KENNETH** *puts the blindfold on* **ERNESTINE** *and spins her around:*)

KENNETH. There are those of us who believe that history is circular and that our every thought word and deed will recur eternally.

I would gladly suffer the perpetual humiliations that have defined my life for the chance to be here playing pin the tail on the donkey with you.

ERNESTINE. I love you, Kenneth.

KENNETH. I told you so.

ERNESTINE. Shut up.

KENNETH. Now get 'er done!

(**ERNESTINE** *gropes her way towards the donkey on the wall.*)

Warm.

Warmer.

KENNETH. Cold.

Colder.

'Iceberg, captain!'

KENNETH. Warm.

Warmest.

'Come hither, come hither!'

Nail that donkey!

    (She pins the tail on the donkey.)

Huzzah!

ERNESTINE. Victory is mine!!

    *(**ERNESTINE** takes off blindfold.)*

    (They dance as if in a conga line, having the best time of their lives.)

    *(**BILLY** enters carrying a paper bag.)*

    (There's something damaged out about him, something hallowed.)

    (The middle stages of Alzheimer's.)

There you are, Billy.

BILLY. Here I am.

ERNESTINE. I was getting worried.

BILLY. I had to get candles.

    *(**BILLY** empties the bag.)*

    (Candles. Lots of them. Way more than makes sense.)

Did I get enough?

ERNESTINE. Perfect.

BILLY. What are they for?

ERNESTINE. We put them on top of the birthday cake.

BILLY. Why?

KENNETH. Tradition.

You make a wish and blow them out.

BILLY. Who are you?

KENNETH. I'm the love of this perfect girl's life.

BILLY. Congratulations.

KENNETH. Thank you.

It took awhile for her to figure out I deserved the title.

BILLY. Do you know what you're going to wish for?

ERNESTINE. If I tell you it won't come true.

BILLY. That's stupid.

ERNESTINE. It's just something people say.

KENNETH. Billy, why don't you help with the icing for the cake?

BILLY. Yeah?

Because I'd be an asset.

KENNETH. Take this apron.

I'll leave you two alone.

      *(***KENNETH*** gives ***BILLY*** his apron and goes.)*

      *(***BILLY*** has trouble putting it on.)*

BILLY. Could you tie it?

Sorry.

ERNESTINE. Don't be.

BILLY. My hands shake.

      *(***ERNESTINE*** ties the apron.)*

ERNESTINE. You and me.

Remember?

We made this cake together so many times.

Every year.

These same gestures.

BILLY. Mom.

ERNESTINE. Hi, goose.

BILLY. Hold my hand.

ERNESTINE. I won't let go until you do.

BILLY. How long have I been like this?

ERNESTINE. Awhile.

BILLY. Will I get better?

ERNESTINE. No.

BILLY. I don't want to be a burden.

You don't have to take care of me.

ERNESTINE. Of course I do, goose, It's my job.

Forever.

BILLY. You surprise God every day.

ERNESTINE. How do you know?

BILLY. Know what?

ERNESTINE. I surprise God every day.

How?

Hey, Billy, don't go away again.

(*She holds his hand.*)

Where are you?

BILLY. Here I am.

I had to get candles.

What are they for?

ERNESTINE. We put them on top of the birthday cake.

BILLY. Why?

ERNESTINE. Tradition.

You make a wish and blow them out.

BILLY. Do you know what you're going to wish for?

I promise I won't tell.

ERNESTINE. I wish you so many beautiful hours.

BILLY. Should I play the piano?

For your birthday?

I'm really good, I took lessons.

ERNESTINE. I can't imagine a better present.

(**BILLY** *goes.*)

(*The piano music rises.**)

(**ERNESTINE** *listens.*)

(*She really listens.*)

(*The melody resolves itself, an ending.*)

(*Ding.*)

(*The cake is finally ready.*)

(**ERNESTINE** *takes it out of the oven.*)

---

* A license to produce BIRTHDAY CANDLES does not include a performance license for any third-party or copyrighted music. Licensees should create an original composition or use music in the public domain. For further information, please see Music Use Note on page 3.

(KENNETH enters.)

(He goes to his wife, rests his hand on her shoulder, he doesn't scare her.)

KENNETH. I didn't scare you.

ERNESTINE. A promise fulfilled.

(KENNETH takes her hand, spins her around, he sings a line from the chorus of a love song that is incredibly meaningful to them.*)

(Either a well known song or not, it's central to their romance.)

KENNETH. Dance with me.

(They dance.)

(ERNESTINE and KENNETH sing from their love song.)

(ERNESTINE and KENNETH sing from their love song.)

(ERNESTINE and KENNETH sing the same lines of the chorus of their love song.)

(They dance.)

(Slower now.)

(They're winding down, they bury their heads in each other's shoulders.)

ERNESTINE. How long have we known each other?

KENNETH. To me it seems like we just met.

ERNESTINE. Have I changed?

KENNETH. No. To me you're still the girl I first saw through that window.

Your seventh birthday, I asked myself,

'What is that perfect girl with the lioness's mane of red hair going to wish for?'*

'If she told me would it still come true?'

(**KENNETH** *breaks down crying.*)

KENNETH. It came back.

ERNESTINE. No.

KENNETH. But we are still going to celebrate your birthday.

ERNESTINE. We'll fight it.

KENNETH. Not again.

I'm too tired.

ERNESTINE. We'll fight it!

KENNETH. No, sweetheart, we won't.

(*She cries into his shoulder.*)

ERNESTINE. Why didn't I love you sooner?

Why didn't I say yes when we had more time?

KENNETH. Since I could feel, that's how long I've loved you.

ERNESTINE. My whole life.

'Where is my place in the universe?'

Right here.

---

* Please refer to the Appendix for alternate dialogue for this line.

ERNESTINE. In you.

In you.

KENNETH. 'So we'll live

And pray, and sing, and tell old tales

And laugh at gilded butterflies'

ERNESTINE. Practice makes perfect.

KENNETH. Finish it, sweetheart.

ERNESTINE. Don't leave me.

KENNETH. Please.

ERNESTINE. 'So we'll live

And pray, and sing, and tell old tales

And laugh at gilded butterflies, and hear poor rogues

Talk of court news, and we'll talk with them, too

Who loses and who wins

Who's in, who's out

And take upon the mystery of things

As if we were God's spies'

KENNETH. You have to let me go now, Ernestine.

ERNESTINE. Not yet.

KENNETH. Sweetheart.

ERNESTINE. Not yet.

(**KENNETH** *steps out of time, out of the play.*)

(**ERNESTINE** *dances without a partner or music.*)

(*Just the sound of her feet echo on the floor.*)

*(**ERNESTINE** stops.)*

(She's still.)

(Shaken. Hollowed.)

(She takes down the pin the tail on the donkey, throws it away. She gets the cake.)

(A cake almost one hundred years in the making, and throws it away, too.)

*(**ERNESTINE** might break.)*

(She's still.)

(She doesn't know what to do next.)

---

*(**ERNESTINE** summons her strength and begins her cake again.)*

(She gathers all the ingredients, eggs, butter, sugar, flour, places them in the spots she's designated for them over the years.)

(She measures the dry ingredients, begins to combine them in the mixing bowl.)

(She cracks the eggs, adds them to the mixture.)

(A sleepy woman enters in a bathrobe.)

BETH. Can I help you?

ERNESTINE. The vanilla, where's the vanilla?

BETH. On the shelf behind you.

ERNESTINE. Could you hand it to me, please?

*(**BETH** hands it to her.)*

ERNESTINE. Thank you.

BETH. You're welcome.

What are you doing?

ERNESTINE. It's my birthday.

BETH. Congratulations.

ERNESTINE. Every year I make my birthday cake from stardust and atoms leftover from creation.

BETH. That's profound for three o'clock in the morning.

ERNESTINE. It's one way I can keep all those I loved alive.

These same ingredients, these same gestures.

BETH. The only problem I can see is that this isn't your house.

ERNESTINE. I used to live here.

For almost one hundred years.

BETH. And now you don't.

My family lives here.

ERNESTINE. Deeds and signatures?

Okay.

But this is my rightful place in the cosmos.

BETH. Is that a goldfish?

ERNESTINE. And the divinity within myself.

BETH. You broke into my home and brought your goldfish?

ERNESTINE. We go everywhere together. We're best friends.

> (**BETH** *reads a plastic wristband that* **ERNESTINE** *is wearing.*)

BETH. Is that an ID bracelet?

ERNESTINE. A shackle.

BETH. 'Pine Rest.'

That's the retirement community by the airport.

We moved my grandmother there.

ERNESTINE. Prison!

BETH. That wasn't my experience.

We played pinochle and did water aerobics.

ERNESTINE. Left to die like a dog.

A room with fake plants and a view of the highway.

BETH. Should I go ahead and call them for you?

ERNESTINE. I won't let them take me back.

BETH. I guess that wasn't a question.

I'm going to go ahead and call them for you.

ERNESTINE. Just let me make my cake and I'll go.

BETH. Get out of my house!!!!!

ERNESTINE. Get out of my house!

(**JOHN** *enters*.)

(*Also in a bathrobe, also sleepy*.)

JOHN. What's going on?

BETH. This crazy lady broke in and is baking a cake for her birthday.

JOHN. What kind of cake?

ERNESTINE. Golden Yellow Butter.

JOHN. Oh my God that's my favorite.

ERNESTINE. You can have a piece when it's finished.

JOHN. Just a tiny one, I'm getting a little self-conscious about the tummy.

BETH. The cake isn't going to be finished, John, I don't want some crazy lady baking a cake in my kitchen in the middle of the night.

ERNESTINE. I'm not crazy.

I used to live here.

If you let me finish my cake I'll go.

JOHN. It sounds reasonable, Beth.

BETH. No, it does not sound reasonable.

JOHN. She used to live here.

This is her rightful place in the cosmos.

ERNESTINE. Listen to your husband.

JOHN. We're not married, we're domestic partners.

ERNESTINE. Listen to your domestic partner.

BETH. This conversation is finished.

> (**BETH** *is about the grab* **ERNESTINE** *but before she can* **ERNESTINE** *loudly hits the counter with a rolling pin a few times.*)

ERNESTINE. I'm what remains of my generations and I'm going to keep the gestures of those whose light is gone alive by finishing this birthday cake.

You want me to leave you'd better come heavy or let me get back to work.

JOHN. What do you say about that, Beth?

BETH. I'm going to bed. Hope you two have a fun fucking night.

> (**BETH** *goes.*)

JOHN. I apologize for my domestic partner.

She's been in a bad mood since she stopped smoking ten years ago.

ERNESTINE. Billy?

JOHN. John.

ERNESTINE. Where are you now, Billy?

JOHN. Here I am.

ERNESTINE. Good.

We've got to get started, no time to waste.

JOHN. To do what?

ERNESTINE. You've got to learn how to make the birthday cake.

I won't be here forever.

I'd like someone to remember something of me.

JOHN. Okay, cool, let's do it.

ERNESTINE. Preheat the oven to three hundred and fifty degrees.

JOHN. Check.

ERNESTINE. Eggs, butter, sugar, salt.

The humblest ingredients.

Atoms left over from creation.

Look deeper and you'll find the story of the universe.

JOHN. This is so awesome right now.

ERNESTINE. My mother used less butter than I do, my grandmother preferred less vanilla, a touch extra salt.

Me? The more butter, the better. Bad for you? Okay, but I want to taste my cake.

You'll find your own variations as time goes on.

(**ERNESTINE** *loses track of where she is.*)

Oh, God, what am I doing?

Where am I?

JOHN. This is your rightful place in the cosmos, you're teaching me to make your birthday cake.

So someone can remember something of you.

ERNESTINE. Where did everyone go?

JOHN. I'm here.

ERNESTINE. Bring them back.

JOHN. You're okay.

ERNESTINE. Bring them all back!!

JOHN. Hey.

Hey, hold my hand.

ERNESTINE. You won't let go until I do.

JOHN. I promise.

ERNESTINE. A rest.

A tiny rest.

(A rest.)

Time for measurements.

(She goes to the wall.)

JOHN. Okay, cool, so now that.

ERNESTINE. Shoes.

Skip it.

JOHN. I always wondered who these names belong to.

ERNESTINE. They belong to me.

JOHN. A lot of birthdays.

ERNESTINE. A lot of life.

Straighten up.

*(**JOHN** gets a pencil, measures her.)*

(He reads all the names written on the wall.)

JOHN. Is your name Madeline/Athena/Anonymous?

ERNESTINE. No.

She's my daughter, the smartest person I know.

JOHN. Should I call her for you?

ERNESTINE. No, she's not alive any longer.

But I still know her.

In every breath.

JOHN. Is your name Alice?

ERNESTINE. My mother.

When I was a baby she washed me right here, in this sink.

JOHN. Halley?

ERNESTINE. My grandmother

She started this tradition.

The cake, the measuring, keeping record of the lives who pass through.

JOHN. Of course you're not Matt.

ERNESTINE. My travelling companion through this life.

JOHN. Billy.

ERNESTINE. My son.

A beautiful musician.

You look almost exactly like him.

JOHN. No way you're Kenneth.

ERNESTINE. Built of heroic patience, the love of my life.

JOHN. That would make you Ernestine.

ERNESTINE. The only one left.

(**JOHN** *writes.*)

JOHN. Ernestine.

Age.

How old are you today, Ernestine?

ERNESTINE. I don't know, I stopped counting.

(**JOHN** *writes.*)

JOHN. Ernestine.

Age.

Eternity.

(*A baby cries.*)

ERNESTINE. Unceasing life.

JOHN. Our son.

ERNESTINE. No rest.

JOHN. I never thought I could be this tired.

ERNESTINE. Wait awhile.

JOHN. I thought I knew what love was when I met my domestic partner.

ERNESTINE. But when you met your son you thought your heart would burst out of your chest and you knew you would give your life for his a million times over.

JOHN. You are my favorite person.

ERNESTINE. Will you give your son a present from me?

JOHN. It would be my honor.

ERNESTINE. My goldfish.

This is Atman the 103rd.

The first version arrived on my 18th birthday.

JOHN. Atman?

ERNESTINE. The divinity within yourself.

A witness.

The only thing that stays the same in the ever changing tumult of the world.

JOHN. Hell of a name for a goldfish.

ERNESTINE. Go big or go home.

> (*She gives the goldfish bowl to* **JOHN.**)

All the turning we've witnessed, old friend.

And to you?

It only lasted three seconds.

JOHN. Nice to meet you, Atman.

Or should I say, nice to meet the divinity within myself.

ERNESTINE. I'm ready to go home now, goose.

> (**ERNESTINE** *steps out of time, out of herself, out of this play.*)
>
> (*However the actress has been playing age she lets it go.*)
>
> (*Our heroine stands tall, she stands as herself, no longer one hundred and one but also fifty four and eighty nine and twenty three and ninety nine and seventeen and everything in between.*)
>
> (*They say at the moment of death you see your whole life flash before your eyes.*)
>
> (*Same here.*)

(**ERNESTINE** *takes in the people of her life.*)

ALICE. Time for measurements.

MATT. I think it would look stunning.

KENNETH. It's a goldfish.

BILLY. And then you stopped asking because the answers began to terrify you.

JOAN. I have, as you know, remained a stranger to my own heart.

MADELINE. I'm actually going by Athena right now.

WILLIAM. Come on, Teney, It's time.

KENNETH. You remember what having fun is like?

BILLY. How long have you waited for her?

ERNIE. You will not spend half the party cleaning again young lady.

MATT. You're quietly dying, too.

KENNETH. Since I could feel, that's how long I've loved you.

ALEX. Forgiveness, the heart of most major religions.

BILLY. I promise I won't tell.

MATT. We raised a family Ernestine.

MADELINE. Thank you for being my mom.

KENNETH. Fuck it.

People say I have terrible timing, but do you want to go to the prom with me?

ERNESTINE. Yes. A million trillion times, yes.

Forever.

(*They dance.*)

(**ALICE** *enters carrying a baby. Carrying* **ERNESTINE.**)

ALICE. Look, Ernestine.

That's the moon.

It's your first birthday.

One year ago I got to meet you, and I can't believe it, I can't understand the journey from then to here.

I wish you so many beautiful hours.

I wish you wonder.

And grace.

And breath.

And music.

And mystery.

(**ALICE** *and* **ERNESTINE** *look at each other across a century of time.*)

ERNESTINE. All of it comes true.

The End

APPENDIX

Alternate Dialogue for Page 75

The following are optional suggestions from the author for **KENNETH**'s description of **ERNESTINE**'s hair.

Original:

What is the perfect girl with the strawberry blonde hair tied up in the most graceful high ponytail ever going to wish for?

Alternatives:

...with the [color] hair in the somehow symmetrical asymmetrical bob going to wish for?

...with the [color] hair in the chef's kiss French twist, trademark, going to wish for?

...with the [color] hair in the wind-swept side-swept bangs going to wish for?

...with the half-up mostly-down although that ratio doesn't make any sense [color] hair going to wish for?